Pinch and Dash
Make Soup

Michael J. Daley

Illustrated by Thomas F. Yezerski

≈ Charlesbridge

To Jean and Gay, two best friends—M. J. D.

For Torin and Conlan—T. F. Y.

Published by Charlesbridge
85 Main Street
Watertown, MA 02472
(617) 926-0329
www.charlesbridge.com

Library of Congress Cataloging-in-Publication Data
Daley, Michael J.
Pinch and Dash make soup / Michael J. Daley;
illustrated by Thomas F. Yezerski.
p. cm.
Summary: Pinch and Dash's disagreement over the use of pepper and hot
sauce in their soup ends up spoiling the meal.
ISBN: 978-1-58089-346-6 (reinforced for library use)
ISBN: 978-1-58089-347-3 (softcover)
1. Soups—Juvenile fiction. 2. Cooking—Juvenile fiction.
3. Cooperativeness—Juvenile fiction. 4. Friendship—Juvenile fiction.
5. Animals—Juvenile fiction. [1. Soups—Fiction. 2. Cooking—Fiction.
3. Cooperativeness—Fiction. 4. Friendship—Fiction.
5. Animals—Fiction.] I. Yezerski, Thomas, ill. II. Title.
PZ7.D15265Pi 2012
813.54—dc22   2011003473
Printed in Singapore
(hc) 10 9 8 7 6 5 4 3 2 1
(sc) 10 9 8 7 6 5 4 3 2 1

Illustrations done in pen and ink and watercolor on hot-press paper
Text type set in Adobe Caslon, display type set in Blue Century
Color separations by KHL Chroma Graphics, Singapore
Printed and bound in September 2011 by Imago in Singapore
Production supervision by Brian G. Walker
Designed by Susan Mallory Sherman

Pinch and Dash
Make Soup

Hungry

Pinch was hungry.
He looked in his soup pot.
The pot was empty.

5

Pinch looked in his refrigerator.
He saw a potato,

some spinach,

and a bit of cheese.

Pinch was too lazy
to make his own soup.

"The Chat and Chew serves soup,"
Pinch remembered.

He was too lazy
to walk that far.

"I wonder what Dash is cooking?"
he asked himself.
Dash was always cooking something.
His kitchen would be warm.
His kitchen would be full
of good smells.

Pinch put a pepper shaker
in his right pocket.
He put a bottle of hot sauce
in his left pocket.

"Dash is a great cook,"
  Pinch said,
"but he never uses enough pepper.
  He never uses enough hot sauce."

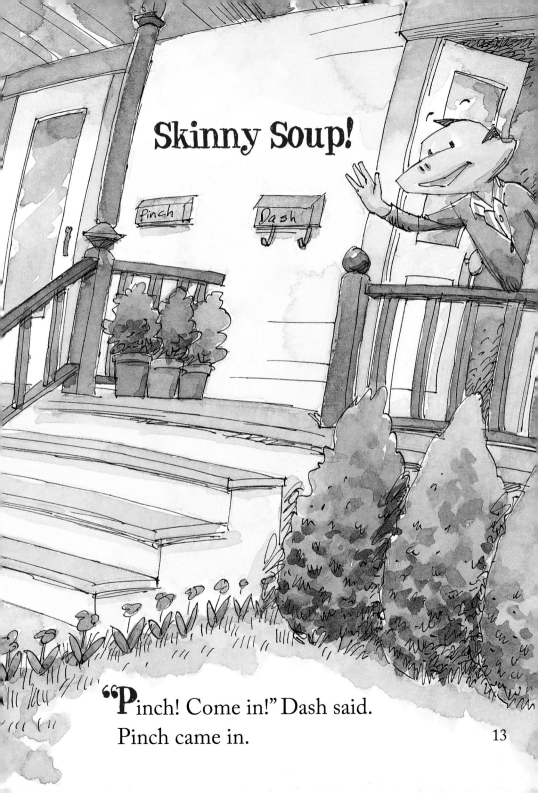

Skinny Soup!

Pinch

Dash

"Pinch! Come in!" Dash said.
Pinch came in.

13

The kitchen was warm.
The kitchen was full
of good smells.
The good smells came from
a pot on the stove.
Pinch asked,
"What is in that pot?"
"Skinny soup," Dash said.

14

"What is skinny soup?" Pinch asked.
"It is soup with not much in it,"
    Dash said. "Will you join me
    for lunch?"

Pinch looked into the pot.
He saw bits of herbs
floating in a lot of water.
"This soup smells good," Pinch said,
"but it is too skinny for two.
Can you fatten it up?"
"Sure," Dash said.
Dash opened his refrigerator.
There was an acorn inside.
Dash plopped the acorn
in the soup.
"There," he said.

Pinch blinked.

He looked into the pot.

He said, "The Chat and Chew
puts a potato in their soup."

"That is their soup," Dash said.

"This is my soup."

Pinch asked, "Would a little potato
ruin your soup?"

"Maybe not," Dash said,

"but I do not have a potato."

"I do," Pinch said.

Pinch wished he had put
the potato in his pocket
with the pepper and the hot sauce.
Now he had to walk
all the way home to get it.

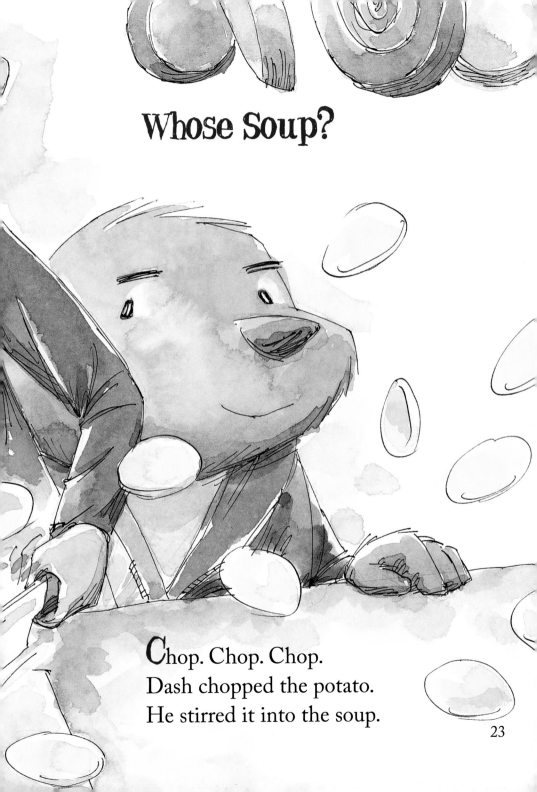

Whose Soup?

Chop. Chop. Chop.
Dash chopped the potato.
He stirred it into the soup.

23

Dash tasted the soup—slurp!
Pinch tasted it.
"Better," Pinch said,
"but I like green soup."

"You cannot have green soup,"
  Dash said. "There is no spinach."
"I have some," Pinch said.
"It is too bad I did not bring it
  with the potato!"
  He walked all the way home
  and got the spinach.

Mince. Mince. Mince.
Dash minced the spinach.
He stirred it into the soup.
He tasted the soup—slurp!

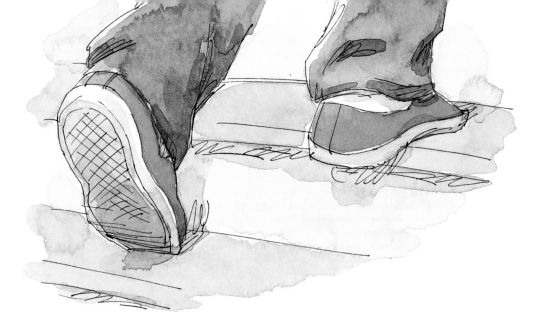

Pinch tasted it.

"Something is missing," Pinch said.

Dash asked, "What? What is missing?"

"Cheese," Pinch said.

"Cheese!" Dash said.

"I do not have cheese!"

"I do," Pinch said.

He sighed.

"The soup is getting fat,
but all this dashing
back and forth
is making me skinny!"

He went home to get the cheese.

Dice. Dice. Dice.
Dash diced the cheese.
He stirred it into the soup.
He tasted it—slurp!
"This soup is not skinny anymore,"
Dash said. "It is thick.
It is green.
It is cheesy.
It is fat soup now,
and it is perfect. Taste!"
Pinch slurped.
He smacked his lips.

"This soup is fat," Pinch said,
"but it is not perfect.
    It needs a pinch of pepper
    and a dash or two of hot sauce."

"No, no, no!" Dash cried.
"Not in my soup!"
"Your soup?" Pinch said.
"All the food in this soup is mine.
  It is our soup."

"I am the cook," Dash said.
"This is my pot.
 This is my stove.
 I say no pepper!
 I say no hot sauce!"
Dash smacked the spoon down.

32

"Now. Should I set the table
with one bowl or two?" he asked.
Pinch thought of his empty soup pot.
He thought of his empty refrigerator.
He felt his empty tummy.
Pinch said, "Two, please."

Alone with the Soup

Dash went into the dining room.
Pinch was alone in the kitchen.
He was alone
with the simmering soup.

Pinch listened.
Pinch peeked.
Dash was busy setting the table.

Pinch reached into his right pocket.
He sprinkled a pinch of pepper
into the soup.
Pinch reached into his left pocket.
He squirted two dashes of hot sauce
into the soup.

Pinch stirred the soup.
He lifted a spoonful
to his mouth.
The door started to open.
Pinch hid the spoon
without tasting the soup.
Dash came in with two bowls.
"Please go sit down," Dash said.

Pinch went into the dining room.
Dash was alone in the kitchen.
He was alone
with the simmering soup.

"I should not have yelled at Pinch,"
Dash said. "I will surprise him!"
In went a pinch of pepper.
In went a dash of hot sauce.
No, two dashes!
Dash stirred the soup.
He tasted it.

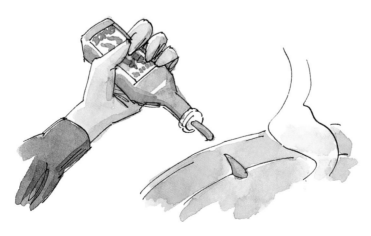

His eyes went wide.
His mouth pinched tight.
"Ee-yow!" Dash cried.

Pinch rushed into the kitchen.
"What is the matter?" he asked.
Dash flapped his arms.
He pointed at his mouth.
"You burned your tongue?"
Pinch asked.
Dash shook his head.
He clutched his throat.
"You swallowed the acorn?"
Pinch asked.

Dash shook his head.
He pointed at the soup.
"Ruined!" Dash croaked.
"Too much pepper!
Too much hot sauce!"
"It's my fault!" Pinch cried.
"I ruined the soup."
"You ruined the soup?" Dash asked.
"Yes. I put in some pepper,"
Pinch said.
"I put in some hot sauce."
"Oh, Pinch!" Dash cried.
"I put in some, too!"
Pinch asked, "For me?"
"For you," Dash said.

Pinch hugged Dash.

"Dash, you are a great friend,"
Pinch said.
"But what about our soup?
We cannot take out the pepper.
We cannot take out the hot sauce."

"I think," Dash said,
"that today is a good day
    to eat lunch
    at the Chat and Chew,
    don't you?"

The sign on the table reads:

TODAY'S
SOUP

CHEESY
SPINACH
POTATO